NO LONGER PROPERTY OF
SEATTLE PUBLIC LIBRARY

P9-CKF-181

# NiNJA

## SISTER VS.

# BUNNY
## BROTHER

JENNIFER GRAY OLSON

Alfred A . Knopf 🐎 New York

We are the only ones super sneaky enough to find it—and unlock its powers of greatness.

# Follow me, bunnies!

**For I am lightning-fast!**

**I am silent.**

**I am brave.**

La la la la la.

Hi-yah!

There can be only one!

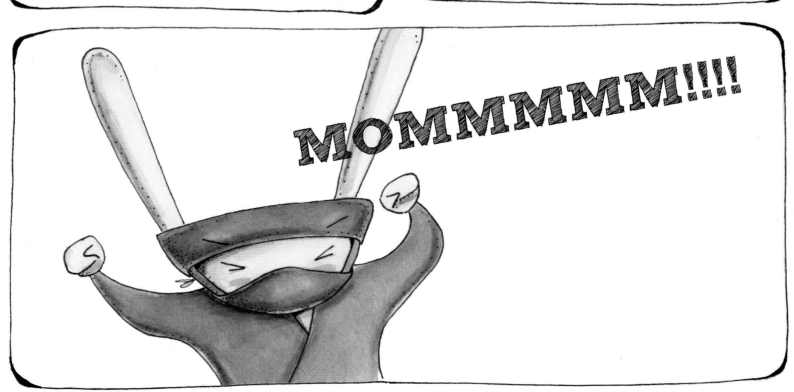

MOMMMMM!!!!

Play
with your
sister,
dear.

But she's too little to jump high.

Too little to use ninja weapons.

Too little to be a super awesome ninja.

Me too!

Only **BIG** bunnies can be super awesome ninjas.

# The Golden Carrot
# of Awesomeness.

And the insurmountable
vines of protection.

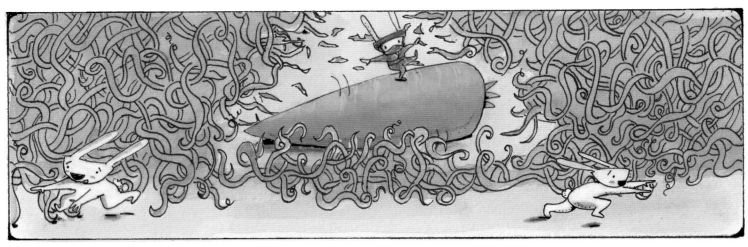

Me too.

FOR STEVE

THIS IS A BORZOI BOOK PUBLISHED BY ALFRED A. KNOPF

Copyright © 2016 by Jennifer Gray Olson

All rights reserved. Published in the United States by Alfred A. Knopf, an imprint of Random House Children's Books,

a division of Penguin Random House LLC, New York. Knopf, Borzoi Books, and the colophon are registered trademarks of Penguin Random House LLC.

Visit us on the Web! randomhousekids.com

Educators and librarians, for a variety of teaching tools, visit us at RHTeachersLibrarians.com

*Library of Congress Cataloging-in-Publication Data*

Names: Olson, Jennifer Gray, author, illustrator.

Title: Ninja Bunny : sister vs. brother / Jennifer Gray Olson.

Other titles: Ninja Bunny, sister versus brother

Description: First edition. | New York : Alfred A. Knopf, 2016. | Summary: On a new ninja mission to find

the Golden Carrot of Awesomeness, a young rabbit meets his biggest challenge yet—his annoying little sister.

Identifiers: LCCN 2015043450 (print) | LCCN 2016009240 (ebook) | ISBN 978-0-399-55074-4 (trade)

ISBN 978-0-399-55075-1 (lib. bdg.) | ISBN 978-0-399-55076-8 (ebook)

Subjects: | CYAC: Ninjas—Fiction. | Rabbits—Fiction. | Brothers and sisters—Fiction. |

BISAC: JUVENILE FICTION / Humorous Stories. | JUVENILE FICTION / Animals / Rabbits. | JUVENILE FICTION / Family / Siblings.

Classification: LCC PZ7.1.O486 Nn 2016 (print) | LCC PZ7.1.O486 (ebook) | DDC [E]—dc23

LC record available at http://lccn.loc.gov/2015043450

The illustrations in this book were created using ink and watercolor.

MANUFACTURED IN CHINA

September 2016   10 9 8 7 6 5 4 3 2 1   First Edition

Random House Children's Books supports the First Amendment and celebrates the right to read.